Katie
and the
Cupcake
Cure

ISBN 978-1-338-89976-4

12 11 10 9 8 7 6 5 4 3 2 1   23 24 25 26 27 28

Printed in the U.S.A.   40

First Scholastic printing, January 2023

Text by Tracey West
Cover and Character Design by Manuel Preitano
Art by Giulia Campobello at Glass House Graphics
Assistance on inks by Marzia Migliori
Colors by Francesca Ingrassia
Lettering by Giuseppe Naselli/Grafimated Cartoon
Designed by Laura Roode
The text of this book was set in Comic Crazy.

CUPCAKE DIARIES

Katie
and the
Cupcake
Cure

By
Coco Simon

Illustrated by
Giulia Campobello
at Glass House Graphics

SCHOLASTIC INC.

Chapter 1

HAPPY FIRST DAY OF MIDDLE SCHOOL, KATIE!

I MADE YOU A SPECIAL BREAKFAST!

MOM, YOU ARE THE MARTHA STEWART OF MAPLE GROVE.

MAYBE, BUT CAN MARTHA CLEAN YOUR TEETH AND FILL A CAVITY WITHOUT BREAKING A SWEAT?

DID YOU GET THE MAP I TEXTED YOU? WITH THE NEW BUS STOP?

YEAH, I GOT IT. I'M GOING TO MEET CALLIE ON RIDGE STREET, AND WE'RE WALKING THERE TOGETHER.

BUT I WAS LYING...

I HADN'T SEEN CALLIE FOR WEEKS. NOT SINCE SHE LEFT FOR SUMMER CAMP.

Are we meeting on Ridge Street?

I HAVE TO GO SHOPPING WITH MY MOM.

AND WHEN SHE GOT BACK, SHE KEPT MAKING EXCUSES ABOUT WHY SHE COULDN'T SEE ME.

WE'D PROMISED THAT WE'D STICK TOGETHER. NO MIDDLE SCHOOL BLUES FOR US!

First Day of K

WAS WEIRD. CALLIE AND WERE BEST FRIENDS. WE AD GONE TO EVERY FIRST Y OF SCHOOL TOGETHER.

MAYBE SHE DOESN'T RECOGNIZE ME WITHOUT HER GLASSES.

HEY, THE BUS STOP'S THAT WAY!

AS A MATTER OF FACT, I *DID* MAKE THIS AT CAMP.

COME ON. I DON'T WANT TO BE LATE.

CALLIE, WHAT IS GOING ON?

SHRUG

Chapter 2

CALLIE AND I WERE SUPPOSED TO SIT TOGETHER.

OKAY, SHE SEEMS NICE.

I'VE BEEN TO MANHATTAN TO SEE *THE LION KING* ON BROADWAY. THE CITY WAS CROWDED AND REALLY NOISY AND...

MY NEIGHBORHOOD WAS PRETTY QUIET, ACTUALLY.

GREAT, I INSULTED HER!

I LIKE IT THERE. AND I STILL LIVE THERE, KIND OF. MY DAD DOES, ANYWAY.

ARE HER PARENTS DIVORCED, LIKE MINE?

BY THE WAY, I REALLY LIKE YOUR SHIRT. DID YOU MAKE IT?

ARGH!

HOMEROOM 2 16

MAYBE CALLIE'S IN MY HOMEROOM. WE'LL TALK, AND EVERYTHING WILL GO BACK TO NORMAL...

CHATTER-CHATTER

NO CALLIE...

HEY, DO YOU KNOW IF CALLIE IS IN THIS HOMEROOM?

WHY DON'T YOU ASK HER YOURSELF?

GIGGLE

Chapter 3

I'M MR. INSLEY, AND THIS ROOM WILL BE YOUR FIRST STOP EVERY MORNING...

TODAY I'VE GOT SOME TIPS FOR YOU...

WHAT DID MAGGIE MEAN BY THAT?

OPENING YOUR LOCKER CAN BE TRICKY...

AND THERE'S A SHORTCUT THROUGH THE GYM...

I DON'T REMEMBER MAGGIE AND BRENDA AND SYDNEY ACTING SO MEAN. NOT TO ME, ANYWAY.

BUT MORE IMPORTANTLY, WHY IS SHE ACTING LIKE SHE DOESN'T EVEN KNOW ME?

CELL PHONES MUST BE TURNED OFF...

AND WHY IS CALLIE ACTING LIKE SHE'S THEIR BESTIE OR SOMETHING?

Chapter 4

ENTER, ENTER, ALL YOU LOST SOULS!

I AM MS. BIDDLE, AND THIS IS MY CO-TEACHER, PRISCILLA.

OKAY, I'M NOT IN TROUBLE.

BASED ON THE PRESENCE OF PRISCILLA IN THE CLASSROOM...

...WHO CAN CREATE A HYPOTHESIS ABOUT WHAT WE'RE GOING TO LEARN THIS SEMESTER?

THE HUMAN BODY?

EXCELLENT! I CAN ALREADY TELL YOU'RE A BUNCH OF BRIGHT STUDENTS.

I CAN FEEL IT IN MY BONES...

A CUPCAKE FOR MY CUPCAKE

IS ANYONE SITTING HERE?

NO, UNLESS THEY'RE INVISIBLE.

HOW'S EVERYTHING GOING SO FAR?

I HONESTLY DON'T KNOW WHAT CALLIE'S DOING WITH THEM.

CALLIE'S YOUR FRIEND?

I THOUGHT CALLIE WAS VERY NICE.

THAT'S SO CUTE!

MY MOM PACKED IT FOR ME. SHE LOVES TO BAKE. I DO TOO.

YOUR MOM IS SO SWEET. WHAT KIND IS IT?

PEANUT BUTTER FROSTING WITH A LITTLE CINNAMON. AND GRAPE JELLY INSIDE.

SO IT'S A PB-AND-J CUPCAKE? COOL IDEA.

THERE'S A CUPCAKE SHOP IN MY DAD'S NEIGHBORHOOD THAT HAS FIFTY-SEVEN FLAVORS. I BET THEY HAVE PB-AND-J.

I FEEL WEIRD EATING THIS BY MYSELF. BUT IT'S TOO MESSY TO SHARE...

THE NEXT TIME MY MOM MAKES CUPCAKES, I'LL BRING SOME FOR ALL OF US.

COOL!

THANKS!

THANKS!

Chapter 5

HEADED FOR THE BUS?

NO, I'M GETTING PICKED UP.

MY MOM HAS THIS IDEA THAT I CAN'T STAY HOME ALONE. SO I HAVE TO HANG OUT AT HER OFFICE. SHE'S A DENTIST, SO IT'S, LIKE, SUPER BORING.

MY MOM WORKS FROM HOME, SO I GUESS I DON'T REALLY STAY HOME ALONE EITHER.

SEE YA!

BYE!

MOM SAID JOANNE HAS A RED CAR...

LOOKING FOR YOUR FORMER FRIEND?

HONK! HONK!

HEY, KATIE! HOW WAS YOUR FIRST DAY?

UHHH...

JOANNE

DON'T WANT TO TALK ABOUT IT? THAT'S OKAY. I FEEL YOU, BUDDY.

RIIIING! RIIIING!

OOPS, ANOTHER CALL COMING IN. GOTTA GO!

BEEP

KATIE!

HOW WAS YOUR DAY? WERE YOUR TEACHERS NICE? DID YOU GET HOMEWORK?

DID YOU FIND THE BUS STOP OKAY? DID YOU LIKE THE CUPCAKE?

HEY, IT'S NICE OUT. WANT TO WALK OVER TO CALLIE'S WHEN WE'RE DONE?

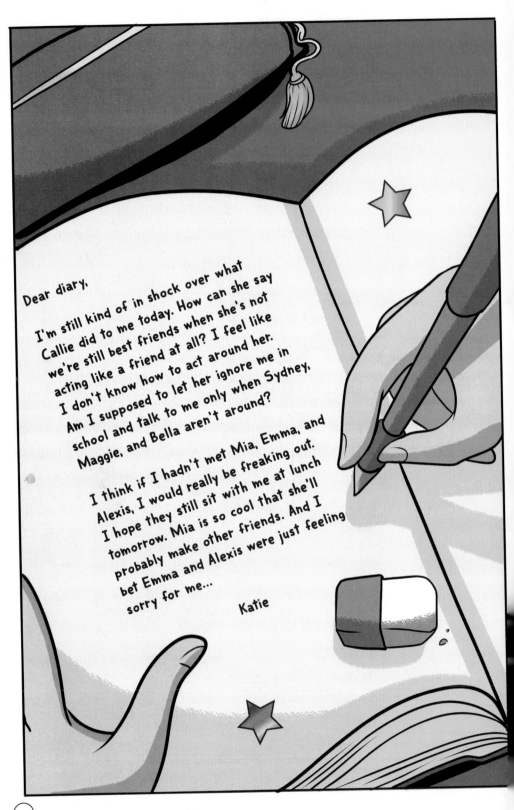

Dear diary,

I'm still kind of in shock over what Callie did to me today. How can she say we're still best friends when she's not acting like a friend at all? I feel like I don't know how to act around her. Am I supposed to let her ignore me in school and talk to me only when Sydney, Maggie, and Bella aren't around?

I think if I hadn't met Mia, Emma, and Alexis, I would really be freaking out. I hope they still sit with me at lunch tomorrow. Mia is so cool that she'll probably make other friends. And I bet Emma and Alexis were just feeling sorry for me...

Katie

Chapter 6

THAT MUST BE HARD.

IT'S NOT A BIG DEAL. THEY'RE BOTH A LOT HAPPIER NOW.

WE'RE GOING TO A BARBECUE OVER AT... CALLIE'S.

ANYWAY, WHAT'S EVERYONE DOING THIS WEEKEND?

WE'RE GOING TO VISIT MY GRANDMA. KATIE, WHAT ABOUT YOU?

DIDN'T CALLIE DUMP YOU?

SHE DIDN'T DUMP ME. WE'RE STILL BEST FRIENDS.

WELL, EMMA IS *MY* BEST FRIEND, AND I WOULD NEVER SIT AT A LUNCH TABLE WITH OTHER PEOPLE AND NOT INVITE HER.

LOOK, IT'S COMPLICATED. THEY FORMED THIS CLUB. THE POPULAR GIRLS CLUB. AND YOU CAN'T SIT THERE UNLESS YOU'RE A MEMBER.

ARE YOU SERIOUS? THEY ACTUALLY NAMED THEMSELVES THE "POPULAR GIRLS CLUB"? IF THEY'RE SO POPULAR, WHY DO THEY HAVE TO ADVERTISE IT?

IT IS A LITTLE DESPERATE. BUT I HAVE THOSE GIRLS IN A LOT OF MY CLASSES. THEY SEEM NICE.

CALLIE IS NICE. I'M NOT SO SURE ABOUT THE OTHERS.

IS IT CUPCAKE TIME YET?

OOH!

WHAT'S THE GOLDEN STUFF?

PINEAPPLE. THESE ARE PINEAPPLE UPSIDE-DOWN CUPCAKES.

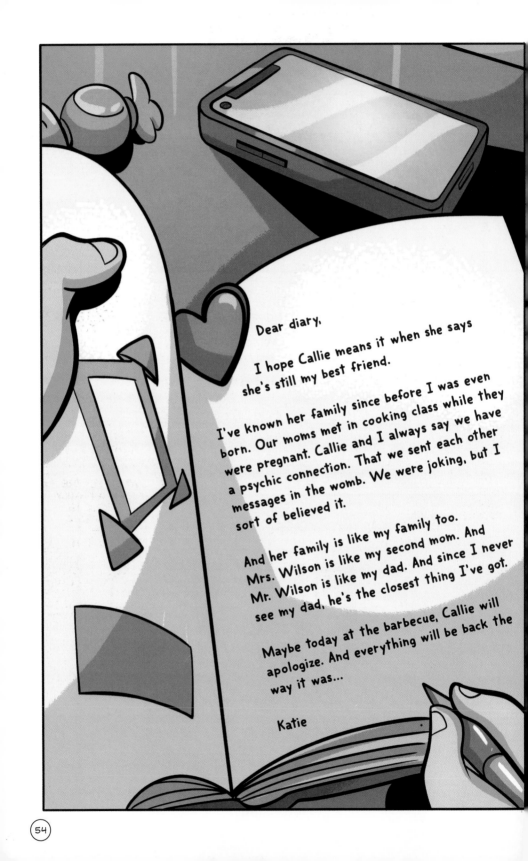

Dear diary,

I hope Callie means it when she says she's still my best friend.

I've known her family since before I was even born. Our moms met in cooking class while they were pregnant. Callie and I always say we have a psychic connection. That we sent each other messages in the womb. We were joking, but I sort of believed it.

And her family is like my family too. Mrs. Wilson is like my second mom. And Mr. Wilson is like my dad. And since I never see my dad, he's the closest thing I've got.

Maybe today at the barbecue, Callie will apologize. And everything will be back the way it was...

Katie

Chapter 7

THAT WEEKEND

HI, KATIE-DID! I HOPE THAT IS FILLED WITH LOTS OF MY FAVORITE VANILLA CUPCAKES!

WITH VANILLA FROSTING!

SIZZLE

SHARON! KATIE!

WHERE'S JENNA TODAY?

SHE'S WITH HER FRIENDS...

...WHEN YOU'RE SIXTEEN A FAMILY BARBECUE IS APPARENTLY A HORRIBLE PUNISHMENT.

WELL, WE'VE GOT A FEW MORE YEARS LEFT OF PEACE LEFT WITH THESE TWO, AT LEAST.

HOW DO YOU LIKE MIDDLE SCHOOL SO FAR, KATIE?

UM, IT'S ONLY BEEN TWO DAYS. IT'S KIND OF HARD TO TELL.

I'M SO GLAD THE GIRLS ARE ON THE SAME BUS ROUTE. MIDDLE SCHOOL CAN BE PRETTY SCARY.

IT'S NICE THAT THEY HAVE EACH OTHER TO NAVIGATE THROUGH IT.

CALLIE TOLD ME SHE'S BEEN WALKING TO SCHOOL. AREN'T YOU TWO WALKING TOGETHER?

IT'S NO BIG DEAL. I LIKE TO TAKE THE BUS, AND CALLIE LIKES TO WALK.

CALLIE NEVER MENTIONED IT TO ME!

I CAN'T BELIEVE WE WEREN'T PAYING ATTENTION. SIX PIECES!

AND I DIDN'T EVEN GET A STOMACHACHE!

WANT TO GO TO MY ROOM?

SURE!

I MIGHT EAT ALL THE CUPCAKES WHILE YOU'RE GONE!

WHEN DID SHE START LIKING VAMPIRE BOYS?

YOU'VE GOT TO SEE MY PICTURES FROM CAMP. I HAVE SO MUCH TO TELL YOU.

OH MY GOSH, THAT DRESS IS THE *WORST!*

YAWN

HEY, CALLIE.

YEAH?

THE OTHER DAY YOU SAID WE WERE STILL BEST FRIENDS. I'M JUST WONDERING ABOUT THAT. I MEAN... BEST FRIENDS SIT TOGETHER AT LUNCH. THEY TALK TO EACH OTHER DURING SCHOOL.

I KNOW WHAT I SAID. IT'S COMPLICATED. I STILL WISH WE COULD BE BEST FRIENDS, BUT...

BUT WHAT?

YOU'RE STILL MY FRIEND, KATIE. YOU'LL ALWAYS BE MY FRIEND.

JUST NOT BEST FRIENDS.

Chapter 8

TUESDAY

DID YOU HAVE A NICE TIME AT YOUR DAD'S?

YEAH, WE WENT TO MY FAVORITE SUSHI RESTAURANT.

HOW WAS CALLIE'S?

PRETTY MUCH WHAT I EXPECTED, I GUESS.

YOU OKAY?

I THINK SO. RIGHT NOW, I'M MOSTLY STRESSED ABOUT GYM.

ME TOO. THE UNIFORM SHORTS ARE SO BOXY AND BAGGY.

FOR SURE. ALSO, I STINK AT SPORTS.

IN MY OLD SCHOOL WE DIDN'T HAVE TO TAKE GYM. WE COULD TAKE YOGA OR DANCE.

NICE SERVE!

THANKS! I'LL TEXT MY MOM.

Not until I talk to Mia's parents. We'll arrange something for another day.

NOT TODAY. MOM WANTS TO CALL YOUR MOM.

HOW AM I SUPPOSED TO MAKE NEW FRIENDS IF MOM WON'T LET ME?

IT'S OKAY— MY MOM IS THE SAME WAY. HERE'S MY NUMBER. YOUR MOM CAN CALL TONIGHT. MAYBE WE CAN DO IT TOMORROW.

SHE IS SO COOL ABOUT EVERYTHING... WHY CAN'T I BE THAT WAY?

THE NEXT DAY

HER FRONT YARD IS MUCH NEATER THAN MINE. NO DANDELIONS...

THAT'S MILKSHAKE AND TIKI. IF YOU DON'T LIKE DOGS, I CAN PUT THEM IN A CRATE.

NO, I LOVE DOGS! I WANT ONE SO BAD, BUT MOM'S ALLERGIC. CAN I PET THEM?

SURE!

YIP! YIP!

FOLLOW ME.

THEY'RE AMAZING!

BUZZzz

MOM'S ON HER WAY TO PICK ME UP.

SO SOON? TOO BAD. BUT MAYBE YOU CAN COME OVER AGAIN SOON.

OR YOU CAN COME OVER MINE.

IT'S NOT LIKE THEY WERE GOING TO MOVE. THEY THINK BECAUSE THEY'RE IN SOME CLUB, THAT GIVES THEM SPECIAL PRIVILEGES OR SOMETHING. IT'S ANNOYING! I CAN'T STAND THEM!

SHE MEANS CALLIE, TOO.

ALEXIS, KATIE'S FRIEND IS ONE OF THEM.

I KNOW. I'M SORRY. CALLIE WAS NICE AT CAMP. MAYBE YOU GET BRAINWASHED OR SOMETHING WHEN YOU JOIN THE POPULAR GIRLS CLUB.

NOT *ALL* CLUBS ARE BAD. AT MY OLD SCHOOL WE HAD A FASHION CLUB, AND A CLUB FOR KIDS WHO LIKE MOVIES. STUFF LIKE THAT.

THAT MAKES SENSE. THOSE CLUBS ARE ABOUT SOMETHING REAL. NOT SOMETHING MADE-UP, LIKE BEING POPULAR.

GOOD IDEA, EXCEPT I'VE NEVER MADE A CUPCAKE BEFORE IN MY LIFE.

NOT EVEN FROM A MIX?

WE ALWAYS GOT THEM FROM THE BAKERY DOWN THE STREET. THEY WERE SOOOOO GOOD.

BUT OURS WILL BE BETTER. ALTHOUGH I DON'T HAVE A LOT OF BAKING EXPERIENCE EITHER. I KNOW MINE WON'T BE AS GOOD AS YOURS, KATIE.

IT'S EASY. YOU JUST HAVE TO FOLLOW A RECIPE...

YOU SHOULD ALL COME TO MY HOUSE THIS WEEKEND. WE CAN HAVE A CUPCAKE-MAKING SESSION!

A CUPCAKE LESSON? THAT SOUNDS LIKE FUN.

I JUST NEED TO ASK MY MOM. I'LL TEXT EVERYONE TONIGHT, OKAY?

I'M SO EXCITED!

DEFINITELY!

SURE!

CALLIE LOVES TO BAKE. CAN I REALLY START A CUPCAKE CLUB WITHOUT ASKING HER TO JOIN?

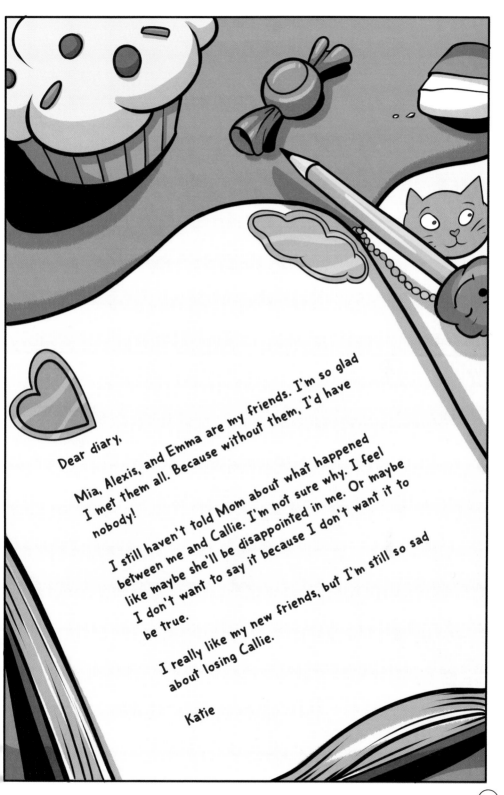

Dear diary,

Mia, Alexis, and Emma are my friends. I'm so glad I met them all. Because without them, I'd have nobody!

I still haven't told Mom about what happened between me and Callie. I'm not sure why. I feel like maybe she'll be disappointed in me. Or maybe I don't want to say it because I don't want it to be true.

I really like my new friends, but I'm still so sad about losing Callie.

Katie

FRIDAY

SO HOW MANY GIRLS ARE IN THE CUPCAKE CLUB?

FOUR. ME, MIA, EMMA, AND ALEXIS.

DID YOU INVITE CALLIE TO JOIN?

I WAS THINKING ABOUT IT. I JUST DON'T... I DON'T KNOW IF SHE WANTS TO. SHE KIND OF MADE OTHER FRIENDS THIS YEAR.

IT FEELS GOOD TO SAY THAT OUT LOUD!

THAT HAPPENS SOMETIMES. PEOPLE GROW UP, AND THEY CHANGE. IT HAPPENED TO ME IN FIFTH GRADE. MY BEST FRIEND, SALLY, BECAME BEST FRIENDS WITH A NEW GIRL AT OUR SCHOOL.

THE NEXT DAY...

DING-DONG!

HI!

91

WHOA, IT'S LIKE CUPCAKE CENTRAL.

WE BAKE A LOT OF CUPCAKES, SO WE'VE GOT ALL THE STUFF.

DON'T YOU USE A MIX?

MOM SAYS IT'S EASY TO DO IT FROM SCRATCH, AND WE CAN USE BETTER INGREDIENTS.

BEFORE WE START, WE SHOULD ALL WASH OUR HANDS.

WHO WANTS TO MAKE A HYPOTHESIS ABOUT HOW THESE CUPCAKES WILL TASTE?

DELICIOUS!

WAIT, I CAN DO MS. CHEN. LOOK ALIVE, PEOPLE! IT'S TIME TO MAKE SOME CUPCAKES!

I NEVER KNEW CUPCAKES WERE SO FUNNY.

YOU ARE LATE, MRS. BROWN. DETENTION!

EMMA, YOUR MOM WILL BE BACK FOR YOU AND ALEXIS AT FOUR, SO YOU GIRLS MIGHT WANT TO GET STARTED. I'LL PREHEAT THE OVEN FOR YOU, AND THEN I'LL BE IN THE DEN IF YOU NEED ME.

I KNOW WHAT WILL MAKE IT BETTER.

YOU'RE A NATURAL!

CAN I TRY MAKING THE CUPCAKES FOR LUNCH NEXT FRIDAY? I REALLY THINK I CAN DO IT.

SURE! YOU CAN ALWAYS CALL ME IF YOU NEED HELP.

Chapter 12

FRIDAY

TA-DA!

OOH, THEY LOOK SO PRETTY!

I HOPE THEY TASTE GOOD. WE DIDN'T HAVE ANY VANILLA, AND I THINK I PUT IN AN EXTRA TEASPOON OF SALT BY MISTAKE.

LET THE SECOND MEETING OF THE CUPCAKE CLUB BEGIN!

NOT AS LAME AS THE POPULAR GIRLS CLUB.

CUPCAKE CLUB? ARE YOU SERIOUS? WHAT IS THIS, THIRD GRADE?

YEAH, THAT'S SO LAME!

EXCUSE ME? DID YOU SAY SOMETHING?

I CAN BRING SOME EXTRA CUPCAKES FOR YOU TO TRY NEXT TIME.

SHE NEVER LETS ANYBODY GET TO HER!

NO THANKS.

WELL, THAT WAS FUN.

Chapter 13

MONDAY

GOOD MORNING, STUDENTS! YOUR HOMEROOM TEACHERS WILL BE DISTRIBUTING PERMISSION SLIPS FOR THE FIRST DANCE OF THE YEAR.

THIS YEAR'S DANCE WILL BE BIGGER THAN EVER. THAT AFTERNOON, WE'LL BE HOLDING A SPECIAL FUNDRAISING EVENT FOR THE SCHOOL. CHECK YOUR FLYER FOR DETAILS.

I ALWAYS HEARD WE HAD DANCES IN MIDDLE SCHOOL. I JUST DIDN'T THINK IT WOULD BE SO SOON.

DO YOU THINK WE ACTUALLY HAVE TO *DANCE* AT THE DANCE? BECAUSE MY DANCING SKILLS ARE ABOUT THE SAME AS MY VOLLEYBALL SKILLS.

WE HAD DANCES AT MY OLD SCHOOL. SOMETIMES PEOPLE DANCED. MOSTLY EVERYONE JUST HUNG AROUND AND TALKED.

DID BOYS AND GIRLS DANCE TOGETHER?

SOMETIMES.

DID YOU SEE THE PART ABOUT THE FUNDRAISER? IT'S GOING TO BE IN THE PARKING LOT OF THE SCHOOL. IF YOU HAVE AN IDEA TO MAKE MONEY FOR THE SCHOOL, YOU CAN SET UP A BOOTH.

YEAH, IT SAYS THE BOOTH THAT MAKES THE MOST MONEY WILL GET A PRIZE.

I HEARD THE BASKETBALL TEAM IS DOING A DUNKING BOOTH WITH ALL THE GYM TEACHERS. I BET THAT WILL MAKE A LOT OF MONEY.

YOU KNOW, I BET WE CAN RAISE A LOT OF MONEY SELLING CUPCAKES. WHO COULD SAY NO TO A CUPCAKE FOR A GOOD CAUSE?

THERE ARE ABOUT FOUR HUNDRED KIDS IN THE SCHOOL. LET'S SAY HALF OF THEM GO TO THE DANCE. THAT'S TWO HUNDRED.

DON'T FORGET TEACHERS AND PARENTS AND YOUNGER BROTHERS AND SISTERS. THAT COULD BE ANOTHER TWO HUNDRED PEOPLE, FOR A TOTAL OF FOUR HUNDRED. NOW LET'S SAY THAT HALF THOSE PEOPLE BUY CUPCAKES—

WE'D NEED TWO HUNDRED CUPCAKES.

THAT SOUNDS LIKE A LOT OF CUPCAKES.

IT'S ABOUT SEVENTEEN DOZEN. WE COULD BAKE A FEW DOZEN AT A TIME OVER FOUR OR FIVE DAYS. SINCE IT'S FOR THE SCHOOL, I BET WE CAN ASK OUR PARENTS TO DONATE THE INGREDIENTS.

IF WE SELL EACH CUPCAKE FOR FIFTY CENTS, WE'D MAKE A HUNDRED DOLLARS!

FIFTY CENTS? AT THE CUPCAKE SHOP IN MANHATTAN, THEY CHARGE FIVE DOLLARS A CUPCAKE. THE CUPCAKES WE'VE BEEN MAKING ARE ALMOST AS GOOD.

WHO WOULD PAY FIVE DOLLARS FOR ONE CUPCAKE?

MAYBE WE COULD CHARGE TWO DOLLARS A CUPCAKE.

THAT WOULD WORK. IF WE SOLD ALL THE CUPCAKES, WE'D MAKE FOUR HUNDRED DOLLARS. WE MIGHT EVEN WIN THE CONTEST.

WE SHOULD DEFINITELY DO THIS!

I'M SURE THIS IS BETTER THAN WHAT THE "POPULAR GIRLS" ARE PLANNING.

IF WE WIN... MAYBE CALLIE WILL REALIZE SHE'S IN THE WRONG CLUB.

I'M IN. NOW WE JUST NEED ONE THING.

WHAT?

A PLAN!

Chapter 14

MMMMM...

TOO SWEET!

I DON'T THINK SO.

WE NEED TO TEST THESE ON SOME POTENTIAL CUSTOMERS.

ALEXIS SAYS YOU NEED SOME CUPCAKE TESTERS?

THEY'RE NOT FROSTED YET. THEY'LL PROBABLY BE SWEETER WHEN WE ADD THE FROSTING.

THEY'RE VERY SWEET ALREADY.

THEY'RE TASTY, BUT I'M NOT A BIG FAN OF MARSHMALLOWS. YOU KNOW WHAT MAKES ME HAPPY? A PLAIN VANILLA CUPCAKE.

JUST LIKE CALLIE'S DAD...

I THINK THAT'S A PARENT THING. PARENTS LIKE VANILLA CUPCAKES.

AND PARENTS ARE A BIG PART OF OUR CUSTOMER BASE.

BUT PLAIN VANILLA CUPCAKES ARE SO BORING! WE NEED OUR CUPCAKES TO BE EXTRA SPECIAL, SO EVERYONE WANTS THEM.

WELL, MAYBE THEY COULD LOOK SPECIAL.

WHAT DO YOU MEAN?

WELL, THIS IS A SCHOOL FUNDRAISER, RIGHT? MAYBE THEY COULD BE THE SCHOOL COLORS.

MRS. BECKER, MAY I PLEASE HAVE TWO BOWLS?

MAKE THAT ONE BLUER.

PERFECT! PARK STREET COLORS!

DO YOUR MAGIC.

EIGHT DAYS BEFORE THE DANCE

OKAY, I'VE MADE A CHART OF OUR BAKING PLAN.

DATE/SUPPLIES/DOZENS

TUESDAY/Katie/

WEDNESDAY/Alexis/

THURSDAY/Emma/

FRIDAY/Mia/

SATURDAY/KAEM (frosting)/

ALL THE BAKING WILL BE DONE AT KATIE'S HOUSE.

AND WE'LL TAKE TURNS BRINGING SUPPLIES. SATURDAY WE'LL ALL BRING STUFF TO MAKE THE FROSTING.

YOU'RE DOING A BAKE SALE FOR THE FUNDRAISER? NOW *THAT'S* REALLY ORIGINAL.

BAKE SALES ARE SO BORING!

IT TAKES A LOT LONGER TO BAKE CUPCAKES THAN I THOUGHT.

HA-HA!

YOU KNOW WHAT'S BORING AND UNORIGINAL? FOLLOWING SYDNEY AROUND AND REPEATING EVERYTHING SHE SAYS LIKE A PARROT.

EVERYBODY LIKES CUPCAKES. WHAT'S THE POPULAR GIRLS CLUB DOING?

IT'S TOP SECRET. NOBODY HAS EVER DONE WHAT WE'RE PLANNING. WE'RE GOING TO BLOW EVERYONE AWAY.

NOT EVERYONE.

I WONDER WHAT THEY'RE PLANNING? I BET IT'S REALLY GOOD.

I BET THEY HAVEN'T EVEN THOUGHT ABOUT IT YET. OTHERWISE, THEY'D BE BRAGGING ABOUT THEIR IDEA TO EVERYONE.

YOU'RE PROBABLY RIGHT.

BAKING MEASUREMENTS ARE TRICKY. MY ADVICE: DON'T QUADRUPLE THE RECIPE. MAKE ONE BATCH AT A TIME. THEN YOU'LL END UP WITH PERFECT CUPCAKES. I KNOW YOU CAN DO IT! NOW HOW ABOUT A HUDDLE?

GOOOOO, CUPCAKE CLUB!

I THINK WE SHOULD DIVIDE UP THE WORK BASED ON OUR STRENGTHS. I'LL DO THE MEASURING. KATIE, YOU'RE OUR BEST EGG CRACKER...

FIRST DOZEN DOWN!

DO WE REALLY HAVE TO FREEZE THEM?

THEY'LL STILL TASTE GREAT. IT'S THE BEST WAY TO KEEP THEM FRESH FOR SATURDAY.

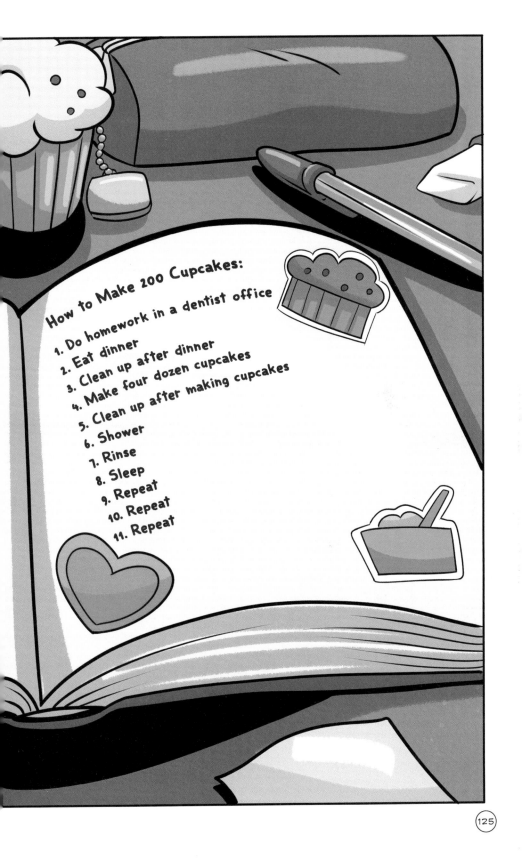

How to Make 200 Cupcakes:

1. Do homework in a dentist office
2. Eat dinner
3. Clean up after dinner
4. Make four dozen cupcakes
5. Clean up after making cupcakes
6. Shower
7. Rinse
8. Sleep
9. Repeat
10. Repeat
11. Repeat

I LOVE THE COLOR. AND IT LOOKS GOOD ON THE MANNEQUIN. SHE DOESN'T HAVE A HEAD, THOUGH, SO MAYBE ANYTHING WOULD LOOK GOOD ON HER.

NO, I LIKE IT! TRY IT ON!

KATIE, COME OUT! I'M DYING TO SEE HOW YOU LOOK!

OOH, IT'S PERFECT! SPIN FOR ME.

YOU HAVE TO GET IT! YOU COULD EVEN WEAR SNEAKERS IF YOU WANT WITH IT, AND IT WILL LOOK SO CUTE.

THAT DRESS IS GROSS, MAGS. I WOULDN'T WEAR THAT TO GYM CLASS.

SYDNEY?!

ISN'T IT A LITTLE TOO EARLY FOR HALLOWEEN, KATIE?

KNOCK IT OFF, SYDNEY.

I CAN'T LET MIA FIGHT ALL MY BATTLES.

NO, IT'S OKAY. WHAT EXACTLY DO YOU MEAN, SYDNEY?

WELL, THAT'S A GRAPE COSTUME, ISN'T IT? NO WAIT— YOU'RE THAT PURPLE DINOSAUR.

GIRLS SOCCER
TEAM SELFIE
STATION

Chess Club
Bake Sale

OH NO!
A BAKE
SALE!

WELL,
THEY DON'T
HAVE PARK STREET
MIDDLE SCHOOL
CUPCAKES LIKE
WE DO.

AND THEY
HAVE MOSTLY
COOKIES, AND
THEY'RE CHARGING
ONLY FIFTY CENTS
FOR THOSE.

IS THAT
THE POPULA
GIRLS CLU
BOOTH?

OKAY, THAT'S DEFINITELY ORIGINAL.

FLYERS! WHY DIDN'T WE THINK OF THAT TO HELP SELL OUR CUPCAKES?

SPEAKING OF SELLING CUPCAKES, WE SHOULD GET BACK TO THE BOOTH.

THE PGC MIGHT HAVE MUSIC AND FLYERS AND GLITTER, BUT WE HAVE DELICIOUS CUPCAKES. LET'S GO WIN THIS!

CUPCAKE

2$

MRS. MOORE?

HELLO, MISS BROWN. IT MUST HAVE BEEN A LOT OF WORK TO MAKE ALL THESE CUPCAKES.

THERE ARE MORE IN BOXES. WE MADE TWO HUNDRED. WELL, TWO HUNDRED AND FOUR, ACTUALLY. THAT'S SEVENTEEN DOZEN.

I DON'T KNOW MUCH ABOUT FASHION, BUT THAT DOESN'T LOOK RIGHT TO ME.

THAT SHOULDN'T LOOK RIGHT TO ANYBODY.

CALM DOWN, MAGGIE. IT'S ALL FOR THE SCHOOL. I WAS JUST COMING TO GET MY MAKEOVER FROM YOUR BOOTH.

MAGGIE, CAN YOU WORK THE CASH BOX FOR A MINUTE? I'M GOING TO GET A CUPCAKE.

CALLIE, YOU ABSOLUTELY CANNOT BUY A CUPCAKE. DO YOU WANT TO WIN THIS CONTEST OR NOT?

IT'S JUST A CUPCAKE.

Chapter 18

HEY, MIA! HOW DID THE CUPCAKE SALES GO?

NOT BAD, MR. VALDES. WE HAVE ONLY SEVENTEEN LEFT.

TELL YOU WHAT. I'VE GOT A BIG MEETING ON MONDAY. I KNOW EVERYONE AT WORK WOULD LIKE SOME CUPCAKES. I'LL TAKE EVERYTHING YOU HAVE LEFT.

THAT WILL BE THIRTY-FOUR DOLLARS, PLEASE.

THANKS, EDDIE. YOU DIDN'T HAVE TO DO THAT.

I DID. I'M MAKING EVERYONE WORK LATE, AND THEY DON'T KNOW IT YET.

SEE YOU AT THE DANCE!

MY BABY'S FIRST DANCE. YOU LOOK SO BEAUTIFUL!

MO-OM!

YOU BOTH LOOK SO NICE!

SO DO YOU TWO! WHAT'S TO EAT?

PUNCH, VEGGIES, AND A LOT OF CUPCAKES.

I DON'T THINK I CAN LOOK AT ANOTHER CUPCAKE TODAY.

I CAN ALWAYS LOOK AT A CUPCAKE. EVEN IF IT CLEARLY HAS FROSTING FROM A CAN, LIKE THIS ONE.

SPEAKING OF CUPCAKES, I TALKED TO MY PARENTS ABOUT THE PTA CUPCAKE ORDER. YOU KNOW, THEY'RE ACCOUNTANTS, SO THEY CAN HELP US FIGURE OUT WHAT TO CHARGE SO WE CAN MAKE A PROFIT. THEY SAID THEY COULD EVEN SET US UP AS A BUSINESS IF WE WANT.

145

STUDENTS, WELCOME TO PARK STREET'S FIRST DANCE OF THE YEAR!

NOW IT'S TIME TO ANNOUNCE THE WINNERS OF OUR FIRST CONTEST. THE WINNING TABLE TODAY RAISED FOUR HUNDRED AND EIGHT DOLLARS FOR OUR SCHOOL. LET'S HEAR IT FOR THE CUPCAKE CLUB!

GASP!

SQUEE-EEEE!

WE DID IT!

YES!

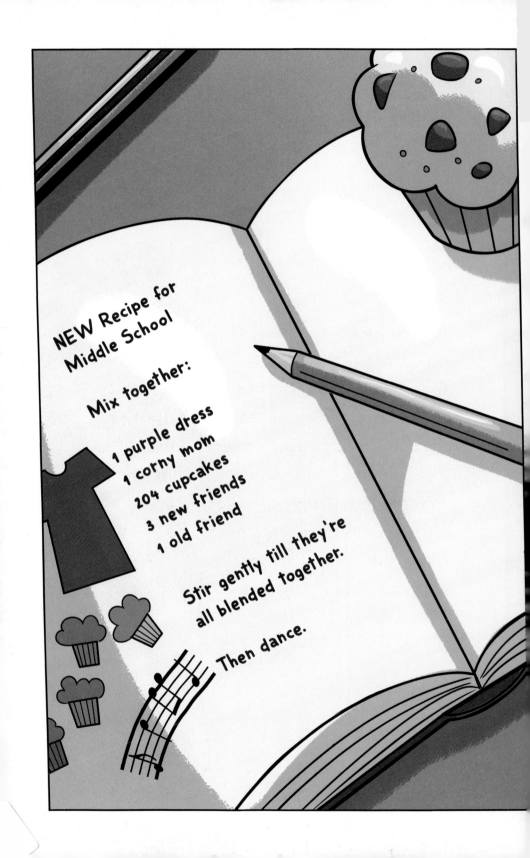

Coco Simon always dreamed of opening a cupcake bakery but was afraid she would eat all of the profits. When she's not daydreaming about cupcakes, Coco edits children's books and has written close to one hundred books for children, tweens, and young adults, which is a lot less than the number of cupcakes she's eaten. Cupcake Diaries is the first time Coco has mixed her love of cupcakes with writing.